THE LOST BOY

A Sir Isaac Story
1213 AD

By Douglas B. Whitley Jr.

Copywrite 2018 Douglas B. Whitley Jr.

Chapter 1

Sir Isaac felt the snick of the cutpurse's knife at the leather pouch looped at his waist. Without turning Sir Isaac reached back his hand like a striking serpent and enclosed the skeletal wrist of a street urchin. The knight turned in a moment to face the thief. When Isaac saw what he had captured his brow furrowed; his lips pressed together. The delight of being at Marseilles left him. Sadness filled his heart. What had driven this street scarecrow to this? The emaciated boy swung weakly at Sir Isaac with his knife trying to make his escape. "I'll kill you" screeched the boy as he slashed again with his knife. Sir Isaac caught the blade on his leather arm brace and grasped the lad's other hand. The knife dropped.

The boy collapsed like a sack of rags and passed out. Sir Isaac lifted the boy gently over his shoulder, retrieving the knife as he rose. He was surprise at how little the boy weighed. Sir Isaac threaded his way through the market throng to the Hospitallers Sanctuary. For two hundred years the Hospitallers of St. John had been tending to the needs of knights, pilgrims and crusaders. He knew they would care for the boy.
The hospital of St. John was a massive stone structure built on the mole reaching out to embrace the Gulf of Lyon. The deep blue waters of the Mediterranean lapped at the pebbled beach in front of the edifice.

The cassocked brother who met him at the door took the limp boy in his arms without a word. Another monk followed silently as they disappeared with the patient into the wards of the hospital. Sir Isaac found the Prior in charge and spoke with him briefly about his patient. Isaac left money for the boy's care and instructions about where he was lodging in the city. His thoughts were still with the lad as he wandered back to the house where he was renting rooms during his sojourn on the coast of France. What had begun as a trip to reconnect with old friends and old memories had become a rescue mission for this angry waif now, but the air was still redolent with the smells of Marseille; the sea, the fish, the spices of a dozen cultures represented in the port city, and the sweetly scented fragrance of the soaps for which the city was famous. It was a city filled with memories for Sir Isaac.

The boy awoke with a start, not knowing where he was. He tried to sit up and escape at the same time, but a hand gently firm eased him back down on the mattress. "Calme', Calme', easy, easy," the voice purred softly. "You are weak, enfant. You passed out in the market. A knight of the crusade brought you in. Repose y mange', rest and eat. You will feel better soon. You are in the hospital of St. John. We will care for you." The monk lifted a steaming earthen bowl from the small side table. "Here. Drink this. It is beef tea. It will help build up your strength."

The monk brought the bowl to the boy's mouth. Henri sipped slowly because of the heat, but the broth felt good going down. After a few sips, a great weariness swept over him. The boy had never in his life slept in a bed. He let himself sink into the soft cleanness and drifted into oblivion. When next he awoke, Sir Isaac was seated beside the bed. The monks had sent for him when the boy began to stir. Sir Isaac was curious about the boy thief and not a little worried for him. Sir Isaac had watched the lad as he slept. He judged him to be about twelve years of age. He was as thin as a twig. With his face and body washed of the dirt of the street the boy was pale against the white sheets of the bed. Sir Isaac could see the blue veins running beneath the skin on his hands, his temples and his eyelids. His skin looked like translucent porcelain from the east. The boy's eyes were circled dark with fear, worry and hardship. His short life had not been an easy one.

Sir Isaac could see the alert wariness in the boy's countenance when his eyes opened. He took in the room and the knight's looming presence. "Como t'alle vous? How are you feeling, young man?" Sir Isaac asked gently in French. "Don't worry. I'm not here to hurt you or bring you before the sheriff. Yes, you tried to steal my money and even kill me, but you were not successful and it is obvious you are in need of help." The boy ran his tongue over his parched lips, eyes still wary.

Sir Isaac reached for a stoneware carafe and poured water into the small earthen cup on the table beside the bed. He helped the boy sit up and held the cup while he sipped thirstily.

"What is your name and how did you come to be here?" Sir Isaac asked quietly. "Je suis Henri." The boy whispered in French.

They had been speaking French. The boy wondering to himself about Sir Isaac's strangely accented speech.

"I am from a farm near Ruen. I came here with Etienne of Cloyes to go to Jerusalem to convert the Moslems to Jesu through peace, not with the sword like you."

The boy had seen the crusader's cross stitched on Sir Isaac's long cloak.

Sir Isaac had heard the news of the charismatic twelve-year-old Etienne who claimed to have a letter to the king of France from Jesus.

The king never met with the crusaders, as they called themselves, but neither the king nor the Church knew what to do with thirty thousand vagabond followers, children and adults flowing across France begging along the way like a plague of locusts at Etienne's heels. Told to return to their homes by the King and his court; viewed with caution by the Church; helped by well-meaning Samaritans along the way this motley swarm found themselves in Marseilles on the shores of the Mediterranean sincerely waiting for God to part the waters of the sea so they could march on dry land to Jerusalem like Moses and the children of

Israel. The sea did not part. God did not do the miracle Etienne had said He would perform. The throng was disillusioned. Thirty thousand disappointed people, some faithful, some just along for what they might get, but all believing God had failed them in some way. How long had they stood there waiting, waiting for God to part the waters; the soldiers, sailors, and wastrels jeering and mocking their faith until Etienne turned his back on the sea as the crowd slowly made way for him to walk back to Cluny? Angry and disappointed with God and the young Étienne, the followers slowly disbanded and filtered back from whence they had come, except the ones like Henri who had no place to go, no one to care, were forced into thievery or worse to feed themselves.

Winter was coming and although Marseille was no frozen wasteland still it was cold when the Mistral came over the mountains toward the sea.

Little by little the story came out with pauses for water, broth and occasional rest.   Henri's parents had joined the throng with Henri. "When you have nothing, when you see yourself as nothing, when you are the poorest of the poor, anything looks better than where you are," his father had said and so they left the failing farm and ruined crops and followed Etienne.

Along the way Henri's parents had died of fever and Henri became one of the nameless packs of orphans that were a part of Étienne's youthful army in this so-called Children's Crusade. When Étienne left to return to the center of France to continue serving God by serving others, Henri remained to beg for his food on the streets of Marseilles. Kindly people had helped him but even the kindliest run out of patience and Henri had been forced to steal to eat, to live. When he tried to rob Sir Isaac he hadn't eaten for days. "Rest here for a day or two more and then we will see." Sir Isaac told him in stilted French. "Will you do that?" Henri nodded. His hunger and exhaustion overcame his anger and frustration for the moment.

Sir Isaac continued to explore the city he had traveled through years before on his way to the Holy Land with Richard the Lionheart, the king who had truly cost his nation a king's ransom. He thought Marseilles exotic then and time had not diminished the city's wonder. There were Greeks, Italians, Turks, Spanish, Egyptians, Africans all living together in this polyglot melting pot on the Mediterranean. As he wandered through the city his mind turned continually to the boy. He could feel the boy's anger welling inside him. Twelve is a young age to be on one's own. It is an age of change, of decision where heart and life are shaped and melded into the man to come.

It would be so easy to foist the boy off as an apprentice to some artisan here in this city by the sea, to throw some coin at the problem and forget him, but that was not the way Sir Isaac believed God was leading him. Sir Isaac knew the boy was angry and lost; lost in countless ways and without care he might be forever lost, forever angry, never knowing that disappointment fueled his anger.

Each day Sir Isaac visited Henri in the hospital. Each day the boy looked better, stronger, healthier. They would speak of travels, of what they had seen, of where they had been.

One moment Henri was a child, eyes wide with wonder, the next a somber young man filled with indignation at things he had seen far beyond his age in an instant this would turn to fiery anger with God; his emotions waxing and waning like the tide.

Henri would eventually tire and Sir Isaac would walk the shore, visit the places he had seen so long ago, search for old acquaintances or pray on his knees in the house by the sea where he was renting rooms during his stay always with Henri on his mind.

The next morning Isaac saw the boy was nearly well enough to travel. He broached the subject of Henri traveling with him as a squire. At first the boy's eyes lit up but then veiled as his anger surfaced.

"Do you have any family, Henri, anyone from your father or mother's family, an aunt, an uncle, grandparents?"

"I have a Grandpere in Caen whom I have never met. He disowned my mother when she married my father. He was a fisherman. His name is Tavel. I have never met him. I do not know if he still lives, but I don't need looking after. I am not a child. I am no man's slave." He said, his voice cracking in the change.

"But I do need someone to travel with me and help me. I will pay you and train you. It would not be slavery. It is up to you, but if someone else had caught you, you would be missing a finger or a hand. Think on that. I'll come back tomorrow."

Sir Isaac spoke with Prior Tivoli who ran the hospital. Henri was well enough to leave, but what then. Without direction he would be on the street picking pockets or cutting purses before another fortnight. How long would it be before this lead him to greater crimes that would bring about his execution?

"It has been long since I have been in need of a squire, but I thought it might suit him until we know what he is fit for. I can teach him and train him. I am returning to England, but I thought we might travel through the region of his home and perhaps find a relative who would take him in. There may be a Grandpere. I will not leave him destitute on the side of the road." Isaac said.

"Sir Isaac, I too have spoken with Henri. He is a very angry young man. He believes that God has failed him," the Father replied.

"Yes," Sir Isaac said. "Have we not all been angry with God at some time?"

The Prior was silent for a moment as if recalling his own battles with God and then he nodded. "Very well, he is recovered in body if not in heart. I will give orders to release him to you. He has little in the way of possessions so at least he will not take up much room."

Chapter 2

The next morning Sir Isaac found Henri waiting at the entrance of the hospital when he arrived; his few belongings tied in a small bundle. Sir Isaac had already settled the charges with the Father and given a sizeable donation for the care of the destitute.

The knight nodded his head and Henri began to follow. "Have you broken your fast?" Sir Isaac asked. The boy nodded, but Sir Isaac could see the hungry look of a twelve-year-old in his eyes. They made their way to a baker's stall where Isaac purchased fresh baked apricot tarts for them to take along the way as well as some loaves and flatbread for the journey.

Carrying their supplies, Isaac shouldered his way down the crowded market and through the narrow streets to the stable where he kept his animals. Henri followed like a comet tail eating as they went.

Sir Isaac had an enormous black charger named "Sebastian" and a mule named "Mule." The pair had taken him across the channel into France. Now it was time to return to England. The sledge was packed ready for Mule to pull it down the muddy lanes of the French countryside. "Can you ride?" Sir Isaac asked the boy. Henri nodded once his mouth full of the last bite of tart. Sir Isaac lifted him onto the mule's back and handed Henri the rough rope reins.

Then Sir Isaac swung into Sebastian's saddle and they made their way out of the city toward Montpellier and on to Toulouse following the Garonne River and the coast north and west toward the Bordeaux region. They rode slowly and steadily heading to the next town, Montpellier. It was seven leagues, a good day's ride, a hard day's walk. It was not yet high summer and bird calls filled the air with melody. Butterflies floated randomly from blossom to blossom. The honeysuckle scented each breath they took. Dragonflies flitted like winged jewels skimming the water. At noon they dismounted near the river that ran along the road and ate the fruit, bread and cheese Sir Isaac had purchased.

They left the animals to graze at their leisure in the verge beneath the cool of the trees. The sound of the river mixed with bird song and the hum of the bees. They finished their repast and started out again.

They rode side by side when the way allowed. Neither spoke. Sir Isaac was willing to wait on the boy and Henri was still angry and distrusting. "At least he doesn't complain or ask me when we will get to our destination." Sir Isaac thought to himself. "That would make for a very long trip." It was late afternoon with the early summer sun still high on the horizon when Sir Isaac eased up on the reins and lifted his nose to the air. He turned his head slowly from side to side listening.

"Yes," he thought, "death. I smell the sickly-sweet odor of death in the air." And then to Henri, "there is something dead ahead of us. Whether man or animal I cannot say but let us go carefully."

Henri slowed the mule until he was riding in single file behind Sir Isaac. They were coming to a wood. The birds had stopped singing. The river was a low murmur off to their left.

The smell grew stronger and now Sir Isaac knew what it was. "Henri, we are coming to some lepers. Some are helpless, some are not. Some are bad people, some are not. They are not contagious.

You will not catch what they have. Do you understand?" He turned and saw Henri nod. "I have had some experience with them from my time in the Holy Land and from my travels. Whatever you do, do not stare.

They are people with feelings and a condition not of their choosing. Slowly now." Henri eased Mule closer to the flanks of the great stallion.

As the two came around the slow curve of the road Sir Isaac saw them; a ragtag band of men and a few women by the side of the way. When the rider's came into sight the begging began. "Help us. Alms, alms for the lepers." They cried out. Some were standing. Others were sitting, some collapsed on the ground as if life had left them. Sir Isaac could see hands without fingers, feet without toes. Those who were more severely deformed had covers over their faces; the women were veiled. Some had arms and feet wrapped in rags, abbreviated stumps of limbs. They looked like mummies escaped from a tomb. All of them smelled of death and putrefaction.

"Friends, I will help you. I have gold I will share and food. I have oil and ointments for your wounds if you will allow me." Sir Isaac called. He could see them visibly settle.

One of the taller lepers let the cudgel he was holding drop to the ground. "Isaac? Is that you, Isaac? It's Holdred. We fought together with Richard."

Sir Isaac dismounted from Sebastian. "My old friend." Isaac said as he gently embraced the tall man who had dropped the cudgel.

He felt his friend stiffen in his embrace and wondered how long it had been since any but another leper had touched him. Isaac turned and motioned to Henri to get down. "Look in the bags and get the bread and cheese. Share it with those who are hungry."

Slowly Henri dismounted; sliding to the ground and silently did as Sir Isaac had bidden him. He moved slowly, carefully, warily like a cat ignoring something unpleasant. Some murmured thanks, others so hungry they snatch the bread from Henri's hand and shoved it in their mouths. Henri began to slice a wheel of cheese into chunks and passed that around as well. Soon everyone had something to eat. Some lay down where they were. Others hobbled away to make a place in the woods away from the road. Sir Isaac and Holdred drew apart to talk.

"How are you faring, my friend?" Sir Isaac asked softly.

"Some days are better than others. Most of these don't know what's happening to them. Even without all my fingers I can still defend us from the ruffians and fools who try to harm us for sport. We beg and eat something most days. There is a leprosarium run by the Hospitiliers here in France. We are slowly making our way there. The monks will feed us and keep us safe among others like ourselves. That's the best any can hope for these days."

Sir Isaac let his friend talk. He realized it had been long days since Holdred had conversation with someone, much less a friend of long standing.

"Are there any needs I may care for? Any wounds that need dressing?" asked Sir Isaac. "I have ointments, oil and bandages. I have juice of the poppy if any are in great pain. I would relieve suffering if I might. We will set up the tent for privacy. I know that is part of the problem. No one wants others to see what the disease has done."

"Thank you, old friend." Holdred replied.

With the help of some of the lepers the
tent was soon up and a make-shift table
and chair from old tree stumps served for
the patients. A lamp was lit and all
was ready when the first of the lepers
shuffled shyly in. It did not take long
for a line to form as Sir Isaac began to see
to their ailments. He dressed each sore
with care and bound each damaged
limb. Some were reluctant for him to see
them though they had entered the tent
of their own accord but his smile and
gentle manner soon overcame their fear.
By the time he was done the long
summer day had turned to purple
twilight and fireflies glowed in the
darkening gloom.

Someone had snared a few rabbits and Henri had shown his skill as a fisherman; bringing his catch to the fire to be cooked. All had something and none went hungry that night.

The next morning as Sir Isaac was packing away his gear Holdred came to him. "Best not mention you were with us as you pass through the town. We are not well loved there and the fear of us is on them."

"I understand. Fear and ignorance run deep for some. I will say nothing. Fare you well and God go with you on your journey" Sir Isaac bade Holdred goodbye. The two travelers mounted horse and mule and continued on their way.

In the silence of the trail Henri asked, "What was wrong with them? Does leprosy eat away the fingers and toes?" Sir Isaac smiled a sad smile before he spoke. "Leprosy takes away feeling. You lose the feeling in your fingers or your toes and then you injure them. You step on a thorn or strike your foot against a stone. A branch nicks your ear and you feel no pain. Pain tells us something is wrong. Then the wound gets infected and because you can't feel it you do nothing. The infection causes necrosis, dead flesh, and you lose the toe, or the finger or the ear because you cannot feel. You keep hurting yourself and the rotting continues until you hurt something you cannot live without or the poisons from infection build up and you die. That is their illness.

That is what is wrong with any who lose feeling whether of flesh or heart, they hurt themselves."

"Why would God do that to people? Why does God allow suffering and famine and disease? If God is good as people say He is; why do bad things happen? Why does evil triumph over good? Why did He leave us on the shore waiting to walk to the Holy Land? Why did He allow my parents to die? Does God not care about us?" Henri's angry words rang along the path and silenced the singing of the birds.

"That is a question many have asked and will, no doubt, ask for centuries to come, I have asked it myself when I saw famine in the Holy Land and thousands dead because of contagion or the stupidity of those in command" said Sir Isaac, "It is the question Job asked in his suffering and I do not have an answer. I know only that God is good; that His ways are not our ways. That He has for us that which is best for us even when we do not understand. That even when life is hard and things happen which I would not choose, God knows what is best for me, for you, for all of us. In that I must put my trust or believe that God is a vengeful tyrant, and I cannot believe He is."

Henri rode on in silence, but Sir Isaac could see that his anger still roiled within him like a pot on the fire waiting to come to a boil and spill over. Sir Isaac whispered a quiet prayer to Le Bon Dieu, the good God, for wisdom and patience with his new charge.

The town of Martques was not too far and there they replenished food and supplies from the townspeople. It was not a large place and so they moved on. They followed the river again throughout the day and reached the village of Arles weary and ready for a rest. Sir Isaac found what passed for an inn in such a place and soon the animals were stabled and fed. Sir Isaac and Henri had eaten the good but simple fare the innkeeper had to offer. They were in a room over the stable.

There was a cot for Sir Isaac and a pallet of straw with a thin blanket for Henri. Sir Isaac had knelt to pray before he blew out the small oil lamp and climbed into bed.

Henri watched him from his pallet on the floor. Sir Isaac rose, blew out the lamp and got into his bed. "Good night, Henri." In the darkness Henri spoke, "why did you help those people?"

"Did no one help you when you journeyed across France?"

"Yes, but mostly I think people helped us to keep us moving. They were trying to get rid of us. They helped us because they were afraid of our numbers."

"Were there no acts of kindness? No one who helped you simply because you needed it?" questioned Sir Isaac in the darkness.

"Perhaps, but I did not know of it. So why did you help those people? Because of your friend? You did not know he was among them 'til he spoke."

"Jesu tells us to do good to others as He himself did; to help the poor, the sick, the lame, to feed the hungry. He told us to do unto others as we would have others do unto us."

"Etienne said he was doing what God told him and yet when we got to the sea God did not part the waters for us. Why is that?"

In the darkness Sir Isaac let out a slow sigh, "Sometimes men say they hear the voice of God when the voice they hear is only their own. Some mean well. Some do not and some are very sincere, but I believe when God truly speaks to us it is through His word, from the Bible. The words I said to you Jesu said to His followers."

"Who can know that if they cannot read or are too poor to have the words of God? Then you must rely on what you are told and if what you are told is a lie then who do you trust? What do you do then?"

"Something you will not like."

"What is that?"

"Wait. Wait on God."

After a long silence Henri's voice whispered in the dark, "You are right... I do not like it." A small smile came on Sir Isaac's face there in the darkness and he slept.

Chapter 3

The next few days passed in much the same way. Riding, stopping, eating, sleeping. From time to time Henri's anger would flare out at some injustice he had witnessed or suffering he had seen and the one-sided argument would break out again with Sir Isaac's soft words foiling Henri's anger. Leagues would also pass without a word. Each time they stopped Sir Isaac showed Henri something about life and living. Sometimes it was how to build a fire. Sometimes how to set a snare for rabbits; what roots, bark and plants made for healing. He taught Henri how to care for a saddle and to see to the horses.

Sir Isaac taught Henri how to mix the poultices and ointments like those he had used on the lepers. Henri absorbed it all like a sponge but underlying all the learning was Henri's rage.

Occasionally at night as they talked around the campfire Henri's temper would explode with a vengeance. Each time Sir Isaac would answer him gently from the words of Jesus or from the Proverbs of Solomon. As the scripture promised, "a soft answer turned away wrath."

But still Henri's bitterness grew. He believed God had abandoned them there on the shore, that or someone Henri had respected as from God had lied to him.

There were occasionally other travelers that passed, but very few. No one wanted to be caught up in the current Crusade against the Cathars in France. Sir Isaac knew Toulouse was under siege from Simon de Montfort under orders to quell the heretics who did not believe that Jesus was God. Battles had raged across southern France. Atrocities on both sides were common with entire villages being wiped out and so Sir Isaac began to turn from the main road to more circuitous paths always heading west and north.

On the outskirts of Castelenaudry the signs of war were evident. The fields had been burned before the grain could be harvested, bringing famine upon an already suffering countryside. In this kind of war as in most wars, it was the poor who suffered. And again Henri saw this as a sign of God's neglect, of His cruelty, at best His indifference. Sir Isaac would patiently explain that these things existed because of Satan, not because of God; because of man's wickedness not God's goodness.

Signs of conflict were more and more evident with the countryside scarred by devastation and Sir Isaac went even deeper into the byways, sometimes traveling by night guided by the stars. The pace was slower, but it made a safer journey.

One such night when the sky was studded with stars like diamonds and the moon shone full upon the earth covering everything in its silver glory the two travelers were picking their way carefully through a wood when a scream shattered the peaceful night. Ahead Sir Isaac heard the scream again and then evil laughter.

"Stay with the animals, Henri. I will see what this can be."

Sir Isaac dismounted and drew his great sword from its sheath behind his saddle in one practiced motion. He silently began to stalk through the wood carefully choosing each step, following the muffled sobs and shrieks until he found himself at the edge of a clearing. Before him he saw three young peasant women huddled together.

One held a dagger in her hand pointed at the four soldiers who were mocking and laughing, the fire of lust gleaming in their eyes. Sir Isaac saw they were foot soldiers, rough and crude. These were not knights. He stepped from the clearing. "Messieurs, we do not make war on women."

"Who are you?" growled one of the men; the biggest and the roughest. Another laughed and said, "It is not war we wish to make with these women."

"We do not make war on women," Sir Isaac repeated and brought his great sword to bear holding it in front of him its point toward the stars. At that moment the soldier who had first spoken rushed Sir Isaac with his pikestaff trying to skewer Isaac where he stood.

Sir Isaac parried the thrust, stepped to the side as the man rushed by and caught him a blow with the flat of blade on the back of his head, knocking the man to the ground. At that moment two other soldiers charged Sir Isaac hoping to carry him before them. Again, he parried the pikestaff carried by one of the men and blocked the sword of the other. They fell back. Then the fourth soldier went at Sir Isaac swinging his blade in a wide scything arc at the knight's head. Sir Isaac caught the sword on the hilts of his weapon and with a flick turned the smaller blade out of the man's hand. He turned and fled into the night. The stunned companion had yet to rise.

The remaining two men spread apart searching, rushing, feinting, seeking a way to harm the knight. Each attack Sir Isaac met and foiled. Again, at a nod the two men charged Sir Isaac together. This time Sir Isaac stepped into the attack. His heavy blade forced the pikestaff to the ground where the tip stuck stopping the motion of the soldier. Sir Isaac's blade caught the astonished man across the thigh and put him down. The soldier with the sword tried a slash across Sir Isaac's side, but Sir Isaac turned the blow and again brought his great blade across the attacker's side crippling him where he fell.

The first soldier was beginning to moan softly and move his hand to the back of his head. Seeing the man was no threat, Sir Isaac knelt down by the second soldier who was trying to staunch the blood from his thigh.

Fear gripped the man as he thought Sir Isaac was going to kill him, but Sir Isaac pulled the man's belt from his waist, wrapped it around his thigh and stopped the bleeding. "This will hold 'til you get some help," said Sir Isaac as he went on to the other soldier. His wound was greater. Sir Isaac tore the man's tunic from his body, doubled it over itself and again with the man's own belt wound it around the slash in his side. Sir Isaac went to the first dazed attacker and roughly picked him up.

"See to your friends. If they do not receive help soon they will die or at least loose much blood. Do you understand?" The man nodded feebly and helped his companions to slink away. When Sir Isaac looked back to see if the three ladies were unharmed they were gone. They had escaped in the darkness during the fight. Henri who had followed Sir Isaac stood there mouth agape alone in the silver moonlight. "We do not make war on women. We do not hurt women. We do not strike them. We do not force ourselves upon them. Do you understand?" breathed Sir Isaac hoarsely. "Do you understand that?"
"You fought four men. You fought four men alone and beat them." Said Henri.

"Yes, but they weren't very brave, very smart or even very good at fighting" said Sir Isaac.

Then a look of bitterness came on Henri's face. "What happened to the command of Jesu to turn the other cheek? You are just like all the rest using force to get what you want."

Sir Isaac sighed deeply. "If the attack had been on me, if they were taunting me or even spoiling for a fight with me I would have defended myself, but ultimately turned the other cheek, but I am to help the weak. I am to defend the defenseless. I am to fight if need be to protect them. Do you see the difference?"

"These are just words to justify war and fighting; the evil of which you speak." said Henri.

"Do you know the stories about King David from the Bible? David and Goliath, David and the lion and the bear? David fought Goliath not to defend himself, but to defend his nation and because Goliath had mocked God. David killed the lion and the bear not because he wanted a trophy, but because they were attacking his father's sheep. I fought those men, not because I love to fight, but to defend those ladies, my Father's sheep; his lambs. Do you begin to see the difference?"

Henri turned and stalked away through the wood back to where he had tethered the animals. They mounted and rode on a little further while the moon was up and then made camp. Henri did not speak again that night as they set up camp and ate a little bread and cheese, but Sir Isaac could see Henri was thinking on his words.

In two days they had passed through Castelsarrasin, literally the castle built by the Saracens when they controlled southern France ages ago. Then came Agen in two more days riding, they passed a few merchants and small caravans carrying wares and supplies from the coast.

Sir Isaac never passed a beggar without giving him something, bread for one, cheese for another, a coin, even ones Henri thought were just posing. At Port Sainte Marie Sir Isaac left the path of the river to take the pilgrim way into Mossaic to visit the Abbey of St. Peter there. It was a magnificent structure still under construction. It was on the pilgrim pathway from Rome into Spain and a spot he had longed to see.

"Why are we turning from the river?" Henri asked.

"Did you ever hear of the Abbey of St. Peter here in France?" responded Sir Isaac.

"No. Should I have heard of it?"

"I was just asking, Henri. I wondered if perhaps Etienne had spoken of it. I have heard it is a wonder to see. We will camp for the night here by the side of the road and come to the church in the morning. I am told that is the hour to see the doorway of the church."

They made camp again in the cooling shelter of the trees for now it was midsummer and the days were swelteringly hot. It was late, but the sun was still bright in the sky. There was a stream nearby where they watered the animals and themselves. Henri lit a fire as Sir Isaac had taught him. They ate a partridge Sir Isaac had brought down with his bow while the bird scurried through the low brush. There was some watercress with olive oil and a pinch of salt as well.

They ate and slept and with the coming of the dawn were up and on their way again as they had been now for nearly two weeks.

As they rode Henri asked, "Why are you going to this place? Do you seek absolution, forgiveness? Do you seek justification for your fighting, your weapons, the killing you have done? Are you going to leave me here, your duty satisfied?" The words came out in an angry tumble, each question more harsh than the last until the words were a growl. Hot tears filled Henri's eyes. His face was a mask of anger and bitterness. His fists were clenched together and the veins stood out on his forehead and neck. His body shook with anger.

Sir Isaac stopped Sebastian. Mule stopped too out of habit. Sir Isaac got down from his horse and advanced toward Henri. Henri slid down from Mule and rushed toward Sir Isaac, his dagger drawn. He raised his hand and struck at Sir Isaac with the deadly blade. Sir Isaac caught his hand at the wrist and with a twist wrenched the knife from Henri's grasp. Henri began to strike Sir Isaac in the chest with his fists, his blows centering on the crusaders' cross embroidered there, his eyes brimming with tears. A growling grown came from his throat as he struck at Sir Isaac again and again until he had worn himself down seeking to harm Sir Isaac.

"I came here to worship God, Henri. No other reason. I'm not going to leave you here. I understand your anger. I too have been angry, angry even with God because of what I have seen done in God's name, but like Job in the scriptures I have come to the place where I can say, 'though He slay me, yet will I serve Him,' where I have come to know what I cannot know, 'that His ways are not our ways, His thoughts are not our thoughts,' that He is so far above us that it is presumption to believe that I know better than God.

Now, splash some water on your face and let's continue." With that Sir Isaac turned and mounted Sebastian leaving Henri to get on Mule as best he could.

With the sunrise they entered Mossaic with a throng of other pilgrims; some on horseback, some walking, several closed carriages bearing noblewomen. There was one crippled man hobbling along with a roughhewn crutch under his arm. There were beggars lining the streets at the entrance of the town and begging children following the litters hoping for coins tossed by the great ladies in their tapestry draped wagons.

Sir Isaac and Henri took their place in the procession. Sir Isaac had left the animals in the care of an hostler on the edge of town. Soon they were within sight of the great Abbey, its outer walls covered in wooden scaffolding as construction continued. The entrance through the Tympanum was ornately carved stone. The two stopped to let the others pass through to the nave.

"Do you see the figures in the stone, Henri?" Sir Isaac asked.

Henri was staring. He had never seen anything so ornately carved before, not even in Paris. He saw the figures at table over the door. The posts were carved figures and every inch was filled with embellishment. The whiteness of the fresh hewn stone dazzled the eye in the morning sun.

Sir Isaac smiled at Henri's silence. "The figures on each side are St. Peter for whom the church is named and St. Paul, then on the other side is the prophet Jeremiah and the prophet Isaiah. In the middle over the door is Christ bringing the Old Testament and the New together in perfect harmony at the marriage supper of the Lamb where He rules as the bridegroom to bring peace on the earth. The scripture tells us that one day there will be no more war; no more sorrow; no more suffering; that Jesu will wipe away every tear and all the things you want life to be will be so in heaven."

Henri continued to stare, to take it all in. Sir Isaac allowed the message of the carvings to speak for itself as the crowd flowed around them like water in a stream. He saw tears form and begin to flow down Henri's cheeks making little streaks in the dust of the road on Henri's face as the message of the carvings pierced his heart. Henri knew enough of the story of Jesus for the impact to reach him. He knew of Peter's denial, of Paul's salvation on the road to Damascus.

He had heard the prophet Isaiah quoted,
"He was wounded for our transgressions,
He was bruised for our iniquities, the
chastisement of our peace is upon Him."
He knew of Jeremiah's broken heart for
the people of Israel.   He saw all his
anger, frustration and bitterness
dissolved in the loving act of Jesus Christ
who died for him. "For God so loved the
world that He gave His only begotten
Son that whosoever believeth in Him
shall not perish but have eternal life."
Henri saw that is was not crusades or
arguments, or even waiting on the shores
of the Mediterranean for God to part the
waters, but trust in Jesus Christ that
would bring peace within himself and
peace to this world. Henri collapsed in
the dust and whispered, "I am sorry.
Forgive me, Jesu."

"Forgive me for my questioning, my doubts, my anger, my bitterness."
The lost boy was no longer lost. He had come home. Sir Isaac took him by the arm and gently lifted him to his feet.
"Come, Henri. Come see what Jesu has done for you, for us." Said Sir Isaac.
As they passed through the ornate portal Henri's eyes were filled with the story of redemption in what he saw; the law, the prophets, the promise, the birth of Jesu, the crucifixion and the resurrection. All that he had heard and seen began to come together in his mind as the good news became real to him.

They entered the beautiful building to find it as ornate on the inside as it was on the outside. The air was redolent with incense from the altar. The light from the stained glass colored the transept like a giant gemstone as it filtered through the haze from the candles. There was a whisper from the worshipful steps of hundreds of pilgrims and the chanting of the monks. The very air seemed stilled in holiness. In its totality the place was truly awe filled. Sir Isaac and Henri stood in worshipful silence taking in all that rang in their senses. Slowly Sir Isaac made his way to the candle altar, dropped some coins in a box and with a taper lit three candles, bowed his head for a time and silently backed away.

He looked at Henri and nodded his head toward the great abbey door through which they had entered. Henri followed Sir Isaac through the crowd and soon found himself outside the magnificent building staring at the massive walls covered in carved stone and stained glass. He realized that at night the light within would illumine the gospel for those without, a beacon in the darkness. They slowly circled the edifice, Henri in wonder at its beauty. There was a small cemetery off to one side with fresh graves from the war. A low wall surrounded the entire area marking the boundaries of hallowed ground.

"For whom did you light candles?" Henri asked.

"For friends lost in the war. For Holdred suffering with leprosy. For remembrance. For myself, that I would be the man Jesu desires for me to be. For you as well, Henri as you begin this new journey with Jesus Christ."

"Could I light a candle?"

"Yes, if you like."

"I don't have any money to put in the box. If I don't put money in the box will Jesus hear me?"

"The money is to pay for the candle, not God's attention. The candle is a reminder to us of those who have gone before us and that our prayers rise like a 'sweet smelling savor into the nostrils of God' as the scripture says. God hears us whether we pay or not, whether we light a candle or not. And you do have money."

"I do?"

"Yes, you are not my slave. I will pay you your wages for the last weeks if you desire, or I can continue to hold the money for you. It is up to you."

"I can wait, but tomorrow when we come back and I light a candle, you can put some of my money in for me, please."

"As you wish." Replied Sir Isaac.

Chapter 4

Sir Isaac had made arrangements at an inn for the night and they returned to the stable to check on the horses before going back to their lodging for their midday meal. Along the way they passed the cobblers with their tap, tap, tapping, the weavers whose shuttles flew as fast as a thought, the bakers with scents that made their mouths water, and the butchers stall hanging with capon, beef and pork for those with enough money to buy. The blacksmith ran the stable. He was at work in the forge when they arrived. The sharp crack of metal on metal beat the air in regular rhythm as he pounded the iron into submission.

The heat in the forge was oppressive, but the work was fascinating; watching the glowing metal come out of the forge, the sparks flying with every blow of the hammer. The iron began to take shape first a thin rod and then reheating, a hook shape at one end then a twist and another and another finishing with matching hook on the other end. The smith eyed his work critically then with a nod of his head he plunged the hot iron into a bucket of water sending a cloud of steam upward into the dark forge. He drew it steaming and dripping from the water. Henri asked, "What is it?"

"A pot hook, young master, or a hook to hang anything that needs hanging."

"May I see?"

"Still a bit warm to touch with your hands, young master. Give it a moment more so you won't burn yourself."
"Why did you put the twist in it?"
"Vanity, young master, vanity, to show I can. That and I like a bit of work to be beautiful as well as useful."
Henri marveled at the skill and deftness with which the smith worked.
"What else do you make?"
"Buckles, wagon wheels, harness pieces, hinges, knobs, latches, horse shoes of course and a bit of armor every now and again when someone can afford it."
"Swords? Daggers?" Henri asked.

"You are a blood thirsty one, young master. Occasionally I make swords and daggers. Sometimes a war hammer or an axe, but those are few and far between for me. I work in iron though I can make steel in need. You want an armorer not a smith."

"But could you, sir, make me a dagger?" The smith looked at Sir Isaac who nodded his ascent. There was a pause and then the smith said, "Perhaps one of these would do for you." He went to a corner of his shop and took a leathern wrap tied with strips of deer hide. He pulled the tie and loosened the roll as he came to the rough table scarred and pitted from the molten torture it had endured through the years in the middle of his shop.

He slowly rolled out the leather revealing row after row of blades beautiful and deadly in their edged precision; long thin blades who had no other purpose but to take life, short wide blades for skinning and gutting game, double edged blades for cutting meat and forking it to mouth, blades of every purpose and shape, even one curved dagger that could have come only from the Holy Land that reminded Sir Isaac of one that had been his for a time. Henri's eyes lit up as Sir Isaac had never seen them before, but then Henri's brow clouded as he figured the cost of such magnificent work.

"These are the blades of a lord, knight, a warrior or assassin. These are not for me. I could not afford such a blade as these."

Sir Isaac smiled at the Henri's wisdom acquired so young, but at what expense. The smith grunted but left the case open. Who knows, perhaps the knight will buy one. He had certainly fixed his eye on the Saracen blade. Then the smith reached for another leather wrapped bundle and with equal ceremony rolled it out. Here were bare full tang blades with no bolster or quilion.

"These are of less expense if you would care to finish it for yourself, young master."

Henri asked each blade's purpose and the smith obliged him with a short description of each. Henri's hand moved over each blade finally resting on a sturdy blade good for defense, cutting and eating.

He looked to Sir Isaac who smiled his approval and asked a price and began the bargaining process that was expected with such transactions. Just when the smith thought all was concluded the knight reached for the Saracen blade and began to bargain for them both haggling for another few minutes drawing the blade out and sheathing it again, looking at its straightness, its hardness, the intricate carvings along the blade reading the inscription and translating it for the smith. Finally a price was agreed upon along with a promise of assistance in fastening the handle to the tang should assistance be needed.

Knight and squire walked out of the shop with smiles on their faces not seeing the secret smile on the face of the smith who enjoyed the process as well as the money he had made on the exchange. After all one couldn't pound iron all day and not have some enjoyment. The smith lovingly rolled up the bundles and hid them away in one of the many such secret stashes he kept about the shop concealed in the grime and dirt of the smithy.

Sir Isaac and Henri reached their rented rooms and laid their purchases on the rough table in the middle of the room. The sunlight from the window fell on the two blades side by side.

"Henri, I have some deer antler that would make an admirable handle for your knife. I was planning on using it myself, but now that I have the dagger it is not needed. There is wood that would work for each side of the handle or rough wood wrapped in leather which we could also use. The choice is up to you. It is your knife. The antler would fit easily to your hand and would be unique. No one would have a dagger exactly like yours. The wood we could choose for hardness and grain if that is what you wish. It would take some care and would be susceptible to fire and damage, but more easily repaired. Leather gives a good grip to hand and also easily changed.

I have leather to make a sheath that I would give you and we will make the sheath together as part of your training. This I will tell you, you have traded better than you know because the blade is good and will hold an edge well. Well done, Henri."

Henri smiled at the praise as he said, "May I see the antler?"

Sir Isaac rummaged through his bags and found the piece of deer antler about eight inches long and slightly curved. As he held it out for Henri he said, "It is from a stag I shot some time ago, before I reached Marseille. The leather is his also. I took what meat I needed and gave the rest to some poor wanderers I chanced to pass."

"How do you join the blade and the antler?" Questioned Henri.

"We could drill a hole which is quite tedious and painstaking or we could cut the antler in two which is also tedious and painstaking. There are hide glues that will help hold it in place as well as putting a pin through the handle and the tang to secure the blade. Such quality does not come without time and effort; remember that for it is true of much in life."

"And the wood and leather?"

"Much the same. We would carve the wood down to fit your hand and fingers. It can be stained with color and pinned to the blade by our new friend the blacksmith. With the leather we could leave it in its natural color or find a stain you like to color the hide. Leather is a comfortable grip, but easily damages because of its softness."

"I think I would like the antler if it isn't too much trouble." Said Henri. "As you wish. We will talk to the smith and see what he may do to help us." They had a mid-day meal and walked through the town seeing such sites as there were to see apart from the Abbey. They walked its circumference once more taking in the stained glass and stone carvings from the Bible before seeing the smith about the antler. Henri asked many questions about what they saw. The smith was once again hard at work pounding glowing metal on the anvil with the regular ringing of iron on iron. Henri wondered at the man's muscle which seemed at hard as the iron upon which he smote. How odd his hammer arm is larger than his off-hand Henri observed.

The smith looked up at his two recent customers and acknowledged their presence while continuing his task. Twice he reheated the metal in the forge to keep it pliable. While it was glowing red hot, the smith took a punch from the wall and with a mighty blow drove three holes in the widened wedge of iron and two more holes down its length. Then he plunged it into the water sending a cloud of steam rising under the thatching that comprised the roof. When he drew it steaming from the water Henri could see it was part of a hinge for a mighty door. Its partner was already on the bench behind the smith.

"You've decided then already, young master? What handle would you have on your blade?"

"I think I would like antler, but we need to make a hole for the tang." The smith smiled and arched his brow at the use of the unfamiliar word to the boy. "Well, I could help with that, but you will have to hold the antler while I bore the hole with a heated gimet. It will smoke and stink but that would be the best way. And then two small pins through to the tang to make certain all is secure. Will tomorrow be soon enough for you?" The smith looked at Sir Isaac who nodded. "And will you come, sirs, and break your fast with me and my wife. We start early betimes to avoid the heat of the day, but my Aimee is a good cook and our hens lay eggs aplenty."

"We will come, and gladly," answered Sir Isaac, "but I cannot continue to call you smith. What is your name?"
"I am Piers, Peter, in English."
"Then Piers, we will see you at first light, which is early indeed in summer."
Once again Sir Isaac and Henri found themselves at the inn after another turn around the city. Sir Isaac had ordered a meat pie for their dinner with some berries so plentiful in summer. Over their repast Sir Isaac outlined their travels for the next few weeks that it would take to reach Henri's grandpere. It will take seven days hard travel to reach Bordeaux. It is fifty leagues and we do not wish to push our beasts too far. Then we will take boat down the river to the sea. There we will find another ship to carry us to your grandpere's in Caen."

Chapter 5

First light found Sir Isaac and Henri at the low door of the smith's house. It swung wide on stout iron hinges just as Sir Isaac was reaching to knock. Piers smiled widely and welcomed them with a sweep of his hand. The glorious smells of bacon, eggs, potatoes and fresh baked bread reached out and drew them in, mouths watering. There in the great room with its low beamed ceiling, fragrant herbs drying from the rafters near the stone fireplace, was a feast, perhaps not fit for kings, but certainly for hungry men to fill their bellies and strength for any work. Three young children were seated quietly on benches at the table.

Pier's wife, Aimee scuttled between them making sure their food went in their mouths and not on the floor ready to be devoured by an enormous dog who eyed the progress of every mouthful. Aimee smiled as they entered and heard her husband's introductions, "My love, this is Sir Isaac, from England and his squire, Henri who joined him at Marseilles. They will be helping me this morning as we finish a dagger for Henri."
"May I come watch, mon pere, sil' vous plait." Said the oldest boy, not yet seven through his gap-toothed smile."
"Perhaps, if Sir Isaac and Henri would not mind and you eat your breakfast." Answered his father. The boy smiled again, showing his missing front teeth and took another bite from his trencher.

"We welcome you to our home, please, sit. I will join you shortly." Said Aimee.

The two travelers sat. Sir Isaac to the right of the smith and Henri down the table in the empty place by Aimee's chair. The dog came and laid down by Henri in hopes that this newcomer would feel sorry for him and slip him bacon scraps.

"That is Barnabas. He is mostly harmless unless you come between him and food or sneak into the house at night." Piers laughed. Henri reached down his hand to the large head and scratched behind Barnabas' ears.

There was a slight pause when Piers asked, "Shall we give thanks? Would you favor us, Sir Isaac?" A look of understanding passed between the two men and Sir Isaac nodded.

Heads were bowed; even Barnabus' and Sir Isaac give thanks to Le Bon Dieu for the food, for friendship and safety for the morning's work. Then the eating began in earnest with Aimee moving about the table effortlessly making sure everyone had enough while snatching bites from her own plate from time to time. Conversation continued with Sir Isaac sharing his travels. Henri from his time wandering across France with the children's crusade and Piers telling of the people he'd met who came through his shop. When no more could be eaten the men stood.

Sir Isaac thanked Aimee for sharing her home, her family and her cooking with them. Piers motioned to his oldest son to join them as they went through to the smithy that fronted the street. The spectacle of smithing often brought business and gossip.

"Pump the bellows, my son." Piers said to his boy. He then reached for a leather apron and hung it over Henri's head.

"Tie that around you to protect you from sparks." The leather hung almost to the ground on Henri. He found the ties reaching behind his back and brought them to the front tying them in a tight bow at his waist.

"We will heat the gimet. You will hold the antler on this table. You must hold it completely still and upright or the blade will be crooked, you understand?" Henri nodded. "I will hold the gimet with my gauntlet and turn it with this bow. It is slow and tedious work for it must be straight. It will make a fearsome stench from the burning bone. Do not flinch. Here, these bench dogs will help you hold it steady."
Piers placed two heavy pieces of stout oak in holes in the top of the table wedging the antler in place while Henri kept it straight. "Relax for now. It will take a bit to heat the gimet."

Sir Isaac stood back from the activity. He wanted this to be something Henri had done on his own, to make the knife truly his. He knew there might be dark days ahead; his grandfather might not be alive, there might not be any family left.

The bitterness could return even with Henri's acceptance of Jesus Christ in his life. The knife would be a reminder of the Abbey, of the smith, of the good in the world.

Soon the gimet was heated and ready to bore into the antler. Every care was taken for success. Piers' son continued to pump the bellows to keep the coke fire hot; the antler was braced and held in place by Henri's gauntlet covered hands. Piers quickly drew the gimet from the fire, its tip glowing red. He held it in his own gauntlet and looped the leather cord of the bow around the shaft of the bit. With care and precision Piers placed the tip in the center of the antler lining it up with a practiced eye. It was plumb on each side. The tip bit into the antler and began to turn with the sawing motion of the bow boring ever so slowly into the bone; The smoke rising out of the antler's end.

It eddied toward Sir Isaac and in a moment he was on the battlefield again with the smell of burning flesh and bone filling his mind. He felt the fatigue that comes after the battle.

He remembered the shouts of the attacker and the screams of the fallen. His mouth was dry with the weight of memory that never left him. This was his burden, his thorn in the flesh. That was the way of war, even for the outwardly unscathed, even for the victorious. It left its own scars that never went away. It was a part of who he was. It was the reason he followed Jesus now in a way he had never followed before. It was the why of doing good to others.

It was a part of his healing. He shook himself to clear his head even as Piers readied the gimet for another plunge into the antler. Sir Isaac took down a ladle from the wall and dipped it into the bucket of clean water nearby. He drank slowly, feeling the cool water slide down his throat. When the smoke rose again from the antler he was ready to watch the smith and the boys work their magic.

It was done. The hole was bored to fit the length of the tang in the blade. Now two smaller holes must be drilled through the antler from the side to hold the pins that would secure the blade to the antler. This was quickly done with a smaller bit, more like a large needle. Then the smith took the blade and slid the tang inside the length of antler.

With a fine awl he marked the passage of the pin through the antler and pulled the blade out, careful not to erase the mark. Again, a bit was heated and driven through the tang of the blade at each mark.

"We will let that rest a moment as well as ourselves. Boys, if you go quietly through the house I think there may be something for you in the great room." The boys took off like lightening. Piers turned to Sir Isaac. "Are you all right, my brother? I saw you blanch when the smoke started. War memories come back to you?" Sir Isaac nodded. "Me too, every time. It doesn't matter how many times I've worked with antler or bone, the smell always brings me back. When I was younger, before Aimee and the children, I was a warrior.

I made weapons for battle and used my own blades to fight. I was fortunate to survive. Even though I fought in a righteous cause, I was not righteous. That came later. Wars must be fought. Tyrants must be opposed, the innocent defended, but it comes with a cost to those who do battle. They may become lost in the darkness themselves or so scarred they are useless. We are fortunate we two that Le Bon Dieu has shown us the way to walk." At that moment the boys came back with fresh bread and honey for the two men. Their own mouths were still too filled with the sticky treat to speak. The two men laughed and sat to eat their own sweet extravagance.

At work again on the blade, Piers stirred a thickened paste in an iron pot by the forge. Sir Isaac knew this was hide glue. Piers slipped the quilion over the tang seating it on the cannelure, the thickest part of the dagger blade. Then he poured the hot glue into the hole they had bored earlier in the antler. Quickly he plunged the tang into the hole.

The excess glue pushed out through the smaller holes through the handle and oozed out the top around the quilion. Piers wiped the glue away with a piece of cloth and placed the entire dagger on his bench turning the vice to seat the blade tightly in the handle.

"There! We will let that set for a bit and then drive the pins through the blade and flare them to hold in place. I think we are finished for today. I had planned to take my boys fishing to give Aimee a break this afternoon. Would you care to join us? And we will eat what we catch for dinner, assuming we catch anything." Growled Piers.

"Only if you will allow me to make up for any deficiencies at the fishmonger and help grill our catch over the fire. Henri is quite a good fisherman himself so perhaps it won't be a hopeless endeavor. Although I do not undertake to fill Barnabas' slavering maw." Sir Isaac laughed.

The five of them made their way down to the river that ran through the town and followed a path Piers trod with familiar ease until they had gone some distance up river where there were no people to be seen. Here there was a small tributary that joined the main body of water. Piers led them up this a little way until he came to a stop at a deep green pool by a large boulder that had obviously been pushed there by a long forgotten flood. Here they made ready and soon with baited hooks fashioned by Piers himself they began to make good on the promise of fish for dinner. The floats were being pulled under by hungry fish and the two men were busy taking small perch off the hooks for the two youngest.

Most of them they threw back to await another time, but there were a few of eating size that they kept in a rush basket let down into the water to keep the fish fresh. Soon Henri was comfortable taking the catch off for the other young ones and Piers motioned to Sir Isaac to follow him. The two men eased through the brush that grew by the rampant stream.

The sound of faster water could be heard now over the wind through the verdant leaves. Piers slowed and motioned to Sir Isaac to be very quiet. Piers carried two long poles made from willow. There was no float attached. The line was the finest Sir Isaac had ever seen. He saw a wisp of color at the end.

"Have you ever tried fishing with a snare instead of bait?" Piers asked.

"No, but I have seen it practiced in the east. Will the fish truly be caught?"

"It is not so much about catching as matching wits with the fish. It is to see if you can fool the fish into catching himself. You must be very quiet. Trout are more wily than bass or tench or perch. The snare must be presented as if a hatchling fly were landing on the water. Do you see the small pool below the eddy in the rapids?"

"Yes, but surely that is too small to hold a fish."

"We will see." said Piers.

With that Piers eased quietly near the stream staying low and moving slowly as if he were stalking a deer. By the time he reached the edge of the water he was on his knees. He began to slowly whip the rod and line until the colorful snare was stretched out the full length of the silk line. It did look like an insect on the wing. Then he let it float gently down to the top of the small pool. In an instant the water exploded and with a jerk Piers began pulling the fish steadily toward the shore as it jumped and fought. He kept the rod elevated and the tension tight on the line until at last the gasping trout lay on the grass beside him. He looked up at Sir Isaac and smiled. "Want to give it a try?"

Sir Isaac cautiously eased down to the water's edge with Piers. "Try the next little pool up the stream where the rocks form a break to the water." Sir Isaac emulated Piers in his stealthy movement cutting away from the stream and then coming back just above the pool the size of a wagon's wheel. He whipped the air slowly letting the slender line flow and ebb reaching its zenith and then he let it settle just as he had seen Piers do. Nothing. "Try again" Piers called in a hoarse whisper.

Sir Isaac pulled the line from the water and again whipped it back and forth letting it land softly on the water in the lee of the stone. No sooner had the snare with the scarlet wool and feathers touched the water than it exploded just as it had with Piers. The rod was almost jerked from his hand it was so sudden. He pulled so hard it almost brought the silver streak out of the water. He backed up until the fish was landed. He looked at Piers with a grin on his face, his hands shaking. "Come; let's check on the young ones. We've had our excitement for the day" Piers called. The two men in happy companionship slipped slowly back through the bracken to where the boys stood on the bank eyeing their floats for any sign of a fish.

Piers' youngest, Estephe, was staring closely at the water trying to pierce its depths. At that moment his pole gave a mighty jolt as his float disappeared. He lost his balance and went in the deep pool of dark green water. He sank like a stone.

The two men started to tear through the undergrowth but as quick as a thought Henri dropped his pole and dived in after the young boy. Both disappeared beneath the surface.

Now the men stood on the shore waiting; each afraid to go in lest one of the boys should be struck and make matters worse. After what seemed an eternity, Henri surfaced with the young boy limp in his arms.

There was blood coming from a gash on the young one's forehead from a stone in the water. Sir Isaac grasped Henri and helped them both to the bank. Henri's grip on the limp body never wavered. Estephe wasn't breathing. Piers was on his knees holding his son to him.
In what seemed like a heartless action Sir Isaac ripped the boy from Piers arms and held the child up by his ankles shaking him up and down. The water poured from his mouth and then with a cough and a sputter the boy took a gasping breath and began to cry.
Sir Isaac returned him gently to his father who looked at him with wonder. "I've got you. I've got you now. It's all right. You are all right. Shall we call you Lazarus instead of Estephe? You have been raised from the dead."

"Oh, Papa, I lost the fish" were the first words from Estephe's mouth and they all began to laugh.

"Let's get you dry, young one" his father said and they gathered up their belongings and the basket of fish now filled and made their way back to the smith's home. When Aimee greeted them at the door Estephe said, "Mama, we have had an adventure." She looked up at her husband who smiled weakly and began to relate what had occurred. She grabbed up her boy wet as he was and kissed him. Then she wrapped her arm around Sir Isaac and hugged him to her.

"Thank you, Monsieur, Merci for the life of my boy." Then she hugged Henri even more tightly and said to him, "you have done a brave thing today. Today you are a hero. Today you have saved my boy. Today you risked your own life to save his." Henri blushed beet red and suddenly became very interested in the floor.

They dined that night on fish in a rich garlic sauce with onions, potatoes, zucchini, apples and fresh bread with golden cheese. Henri got the biggest piece of fish, the trout caught by Sir Isaac and everyone ate their fill. There were jests and laughter, stories and tales; an evening of joy arising from what could have been.

That night in the darkness of their room when the two travelers had turned in for the night Henri broke the stillness, "I did not set out to be brave or risk my life. Estephe just went in and I went in after him. I just did it."

"That is the way of bravery, Henri. One does not set out to be brave. Something happens and you act from what is inside you. Helping, saving, rescuing, come from the heart. The scriptures speak of 'out of the heart a man speaketh' but I think out of his heart he acts as well."

"So that is why you fought? That is why you helped your friend, Holdred and those lepers? That is why you defended those ladies even though you did not know them, had never seen them? Because it was right? Because it was inside you?"

"Henri, do you know the story of Daniel from the Bible?"

"Daniel and the lion's den?" Henri responded.

"Yes, the same Daniel. In the beginning of that story we learn that Daniel and his three friends were captured by a prince, Nebuchadnezzar who later became king. They were taken far from their home, thousands of leagues. Everything from their home, their culture was taken from them, their food, their drink, their worship and they were forced to become like the Persians. Their food was not prepared in accordance with their worship and for them it was forbidden to eat it. There were many taken from the royal house of Israel but only these four are mentioned here.

The Bible says, 'they purposed in their hearts that they would not defile themselves with the king's meat.' That is what is says in the Latin. So when the tests came, when the trials came, when action was required they were ready to do what was right because of what was inside them. You did what you did today because somewhere along the way you determined, you purposed in your heart, that you would risk your life to save someone else. That you would do what was right and you did. I have never been more proud of you than I was today when I saw you dive into that water and never more fearful for you. Now sleep if you can. We must finish up on your dagger on the morrow and be on our way. Good night. Sleep well."

Morning found them again at the smithy with Piers after another Lucullan breakfast. The hide glue had set and Piers forced the small gimet through the openings easily to clear the way for the pins that would keep the tang in the antler. He threaded the pin through each hole and then with a small punch carefully flared the ends to set them in the antler grip. It did not take long. While Piers was working on the knife, Sir Isaac and Henri fashioned a sheath from deer hide, wood and leather strips that laced the pieces together to hold the knife. Henri smiled proudly as Piers slid the knife sheath onto Henri's belt and fastened it around his slender waist.

"There! Wear it proudly and use it well." Piers said, "And one more thing I have for you." Piers unrolled another leather wrapped bundle and drew out a sword. "I do not know what the future holds for you, Henri, but please take this weapon as a remembrance of our family and a tribute to what you have done for us in rescuing our son. May Le Bon Dieu go with you all the days of your life." Henri held the blade in his hand not knowing what to say except "Merci, Monsieur."

Aimee came in then with her boys, ladened with sacks of food for their journey; cheeses, bread, fruit. She hugged the two travelers once again, holding Henri to her and kissing a blessing on his forehead.

With tears in her eyes she wished them God's speed and watched as the two travelers led their burdened mounts through the dusty streets of the city on their journey toward Bordeaux.

The days passed quickly as they rode along to Bordeaux. Still keeping to remote byways off the main track the two travelers rode nearly twenty miles each day, making camp at night and taking time for sword play with Henri's new weapon. Sir Isaac showed him how to hold the sword; how to ward off a blow and how to attack.

Little by little each day Henri learned what to do with the sword and as he worked at his sword craft his muscles began to fill out. His reflexes quickened and his agility increased.

Sir Isaac continued Henri's lessons in reading French and Latin as well as English with the few books and scrolls Sir Isaac carried in his luggage. Henri learned to sound out the letters and words. He was a quick study and soon he was reading on his own. It was as if he had been sleeping through his life and had now awakened. With all these accomplishments Sir Isaac began to wonder to himself just what he was preparing Henri for; certainly not the life of a lowly servant or even a deck hand on a fishing boat. Not every avenue would be opened for a boy who could read, do sums, fight with a sword and was already skilled in knowledge far beyond many adults. This began to weigh on Sir Isaac.

His only comfort was that God was in control and knew just where He wanted Henri. He had as Jesu had said, "a place for you."
Sir Isaac prayed each night and again each morning that God would show him what was best for Henri.

Chapter 6
Finally they reached Bordeaux and the river Garonne which led to the sea. Sir Isaac found an inn near the river. He wanted to take time to show Henri the great city with its rich heritage, its Cathedral of St. Andre. The city was more English than French. Allegiance was for Eleanor of Aquitaine and her sons, Richard and John rather than Phillip of France.

All around them they heard English and French spoken in equal proportions as they heard wine merchants and shippers haggle over their wares. The air was filled with the heady scent of wine, the chief product of the region as well as its greatest source of pride. From Bordeaux vintages went throughout the whole world. Warehouses filled with oaken casks lined the narrow streets and carts rolled slowly so as not to disturb the vintner or the vintage in this capital of the wine world.

For three days the pair saw the sights of Bordeaux expanding Henri's experiences of the world. They found the captain of a hulk heading out to sea willing to take on passengers and their animals with his cargo of wine set for England. They began their journey up the mouth of the Garonne heading for Brest.
With good weather and a fair breeze, the captain thought it would take perhaps a week, perhaps a bit less. This was Henri's first time on a ship. He had heard of Le Mal du Mer and he did not want to be seasick.

The captain laughed and said we would not be on the sea for a while yet and the Garonne was as peaceful as a lake all the way to the Gironde Estuary where the Garonne and the Dordogne Rivers merged. The lapstrake built ship had the bluff bows and wide stern of a merchantman. It was designed to hold a maximum of cargo. The few animals apart from Barnabas and Mule were pigs destined for the captain's home in Brest. Barnabas and Mule were lowered into the hold by wide bands across their bellies. The two did not appear to enjoy the ride. Sir Isaac and Henri soon settled them with feed.

The tide turned to match the flow of the river and the hulk set sail with the early morning. Henri was at the railing watching the shore go by at what was to him a rapid pace.

After giving his commands and assuring all was as it should be the captain called the two travelers up to the tiller with him. He was proud of his ship and eager to talk to the English knight about his travels in the east.

The flat-bottomed ship sailed on league after league throughout the day passing smaller tributaries into the river. The cities swept by in a blur all running together in Henri's mind as the captain rattled off commentary and memory with each place. He spoke of heavy weather, fog, damage and hardship with equal enthusiasm.

The sun shone hot on the summer's day. The smells of the stone washed deck, the pitch in the moss filled seams keeping out the water combined with the aromas that wafted out to meet them from the cities of the shore made sailing a feast for the senses. The great square sail hummed with the breeze.

The water plashed as the bow cut the river and burbled as it came together again after the iron bound rudder. The gulls were reeling and crying overhead. "This is the life." Henri thought. Sir Isaac could see the smile on his young charge's face and could not recall him ever looking so happy.

The hulk had slowed as the tide turned again now at odds with the flow of the river. If it were not for the wind they would make no headway, as it was they were now barely creeping along in the light breeze. The captain had started a leeward tack to put the ship into the wind as he began an ever-swerving course to meet the onshore breeze that now joined the tide to fight their progress. The sun had begun to sink lower on the horizon turning the water to golden fire sweeping ahead of them as they sailed west. Back and forth the hulk crawled across the breadth of the river using the breeze to keep moving forward against the rising tide. Each turn brought a flurry of commands and a scurrying of feet as the sailors set the sails.

Sir Isaac admired the precision with which each task was carried out and thought the captain a good captain indeed to get so much out of his ship and his men.

Suddenly there was a cry from the look out. He was pointing toward the sun. Sir Isaac's eyes followed the sailors arm and he saw row upon row of large rolling waves pushing toward them. The captain shouted commands and jammed the tiller hard to center the ship to the waves. In English he shouted "Hold fast." Sir Isaac swept up Henri and moved with him to the center mast of the ship. Just as the waves hit them the ship's bow turned to meet the water squarely to the wave.

The bow cut the water like a blunt knife and the ship rose and fell with the passing swell with the spray inundating everyone on deck. As the ship's stern was lifting with the wave the bow was dipping to meet the next and the water poured in over the scuppers and flooded the deck rushing into the open hold in the fair weather to keep the animals from getting too heated. The ship felt instantly heavier. It slowed almost to a standstill as the series of waves battered the wallowing craft. The captain shouted the command to batten the hold to keep out the water. The sailors instantly moved to obey, but the waves continued to wash over the ship knocking men to the deck.

Sir Isaac had wrapped a loose rope around Henri when he got him to the mast. He saw a sailor struggling with the hatch cover for the hold and knew if it did not get in place the next deluge might sink them. He lunged toward the man and together they managed to get the hatch in place and fastened down as the water rolled over the deck. Then all was calm. There were no more waves. The captain continued to shout commands in French while searching the distant shore for a place to land should they need repairs. The sailors moved with urgency to carry out his orders. As quickly as the crisis had come it had subsided.

"What just happened, Captain?" Asked Sir Isaac.

"The tidal bore. This time of the year when the moon is full, the tides are high and the river is a bit low. It makes for higher waves.

We were watching but looking into the sun the lookout did not see the waves as soon as he should. With the light breeze and no headway, we were fortunate to meet the waves bow on. Sideways and we would have broached to. The ship could not have recovered herself and that would be that; as it is we are riding lower than I would like. We will put into a small village with a dock on the far shore until we can pump out the excess water and make certain there is no damage or the action of the water inside will damage the walls and the cargo. It will delay our voyage a bit, but better safe than sorry, no?

Monsieur, thank you for helping my man and saving our ship. It did not escape me. I am in your debt."

"Do not think of it, captain. My horse does not like to bathe."

"Always with the English there are jokes, but thank you again, Monsieur." Sir Isaac untied Henri and checked to see that he was unharmed. "See to the animals, Henri. I dare say their fodder is wet. Get some dry clothes on yourself."

The captain guided the hulk to the near shore and gave the order to drop anchor. The pumps were rigged and the rest of the day was spent pumping the bilge where the excess water gathered, checking the cargo and seeing to the animals. There was no damage to the ship other than wet and ships and crews were well used to that.

After a few hours the ship continued her journey to Brest through the Gironde Estuary to the open Atlantic. For the rest of the voyage they hugged the coast never leaving the sight of land. After five days of clear sailing, the fire signal at Brest showed on the horizon followed by the squat tower and walls of the Chateau de Brest protecting the harbor at its narrowest point. The cliff walls rose sharply out of the water on each side of the bay. The Penfeld River cut the bay in two as it flowed to the sea carving out the steep cliffs over the centuries.

There were fishing boats, cogs, hulks and one strange craft that looked like a Viking raider bobbing in the protected bay. The captain moored the boat in the open water between the two arms of the land away from other ships. He did not wish to risk a fire or an invasion of rats and thieves from shore.

The day was again beautiful as the travelers looked out over the bay and city of Brest. The captain spoke to Sir Isaac, "Monsieur, we will be moored here overnight while I go see my wife and children. My first mate will be in charge. If you wish to come ashore I shall make my barge available to you or you may come with me when I leave in an hour. We sail for England on the morrow on the evening tide."

"Thank you, Captain. I need to find another ship making for Cherbourg. Do you know of any to recommend?"

"Mais oui, Monsieur. I have a friend who is captain of a cog that makes that journey. Do you see the craft with the high sides and square stern just to the left of the knarr?"

"Knarr, that is the ship that looks like the Viking longboat?"

"Oui, he is a devil that one. He is a Viking from the north. She is a fast ship but cannot hold as much cargo as my hulk. My friend's cog is the ship for you. Come with me now and I will see if he is aboard. I will introduce you and perhaps you shall book passage. Then he can come along side and your animals can be loaded into his hold."

"It shall be as you say. Give me a moment to speak to Henri."

Sir Isaac called Henri to him and gave orders to gather their things and get the animals ready for the transfer. He pointed out the new ship and told him he would return shortly with news.

"Will we go ashore here?" Henri asked.

"Do you wish to go ashore here?"

Henri smiled, "Exploring is more fun when I'm not starving. May we please?"

"When all is transferred we will go ashore. I do not know what our new captain's time table will be so our time may not be our own." In Sir Isaac's mind he was thankful that Henri could make light of his former woes.

"Merci, thank you, Sir Isaac."

The hulk captain returned shortly with the news that the travelers would be welcome aboard the cog. They were rowed across the bay in some state in the captain's barge and climbed aboard the steep sided cog to the smiles and greeting of the hulk captain's friend. Sir Isaac felt easy with this new man and arrangements were soon made to transfer their belongings and the animals to the cog. The captain planned to leave Brest for Cherbourg and on to Caen in two days. Sir Isaac smiled knowing Henri would be pleased with time to explore. He returned to the hulk in the captain's barge to share the news and sent the captain eagerly on his way to his family. The cog eased from her moorings and came alongside the hulk. Orders were given by the first mate.

Sebastian and Mule, to their dismay were quickly swept up out of the hold and down again into the cog with much braying and neighing and flicking of tails.

The ships sides were just unequal enough that the two travelers could not step from ship to ship. A rope whip swung their baggage over the watery divide between the two vessels and came back with a loop for Sir Isaac to stand in and be flown over to the new ship. When his turn came Henri whooped with delight at the ride that now covered a widening gap. The sailors on the cog smiled and began lowering him to the water for a dunking. Henri surprised them by diving in from the rope and swimming to the side of the ship.

He clambered up the high side of the cog
and stood dripping and smiling on the
deck. Sir Isaac laughed and told him to
go changed to dry clothes in the cabin.
They were going ashore.

The new captain was a true Breton who
spoke French and English. There was an
instant bond and he too let them use his
personal barge to go ashore. He gave
them the name of an inn that served
good food and several shops for food that
would make their voyage more
enjoyable.

Armed with this information Sir Isaac
and Henri set out to see the town of
Brest. Like Marseilles it was a polyglot
city. Sir Isaac heard Spanish, English,
French, Breton, and African dialects in
the quayside marketplace.

He looked at the Chateau du Brest and could follow the art of war in the variety of its architecture. He even saw Middle Eastern influence doubtless brought back from the earliest French crusaders. For two days the knight and his squire enjoyed the beauty of the city; visiting the cathedral, walking along the quay and hiking the cliffs that surrounded the bay. Then it was time to board ship again. The two were welcomed on deck like long lost friends. The tide turned and once again they were heading for the open ocean. Three days sail brought them to Cherbourg where there was little time for exploration. They touched long enough to trade a few supplies and purchase fresh fruit and vegetables.

Sir Isaac took time to give Henri a little history of the city fought over by the French and English for decades before the French prevailed.

The ship skirted the peninsula and in two more days arrived at Lannion, a small port city where again a few goods were exchanged, but there was no time to go ashore.

Saint Malo was the next port city of call, it was famous for its oysters and Sir Isaac looked forward to enjoying its bounty. The captain had proven to be friendly and jocular. He conversed easily in French, English and Breton with his passengers and crew.

Sir Isaac and Henri dined with him at every meal. Henri sat in rapt attention as he told of his travels and adventures on the sea. The meal was over and Henri was seeing to their animals before turning in for the night. Since they began to sail in the open ocean Henri often stood by the rail of stern to watch the phosphorescent glow stirred by the passage of the ship through the sea. It was mesmerizing in its beauty. Dark nights like tonight without a moon the glow shone brighter. Henri gazed at it with wonder.

CHAPTER 7

The captain had asked Sir Isaac to remain with him when Henri left the table. "Mon ami, we are a day from St. Malo. I wish to stop there to trade on the morrow, but tonight I would ask you to watch with me. St. Malo is a wonderful city, very beautiful, but it is also the home of corsairs. I have been attacked before on this run and it is possible that we may be attacked again. There are watchers along the coast who follow the passage of ships and although I have sailed far from the shore to avoid their eyes I fear our presence is known. We may be attacked tonight. These men rarely attack in the daylight. They are fearsome fighters and I would be easier if I knew you would be with me on watch."

"Yes, Captain, I will watch with you. My sword is yours and Henri's as well. I have trained him to fight and although he is small he is a good swordsman."

"I hope it will not come to that, but it is better to be prepared, is it not?"

Henri watched the swirling glow stretch out behind the ship. He saw a blackness in the midst of the phosphorescence. He stared until his eyes ached in his head to see what it was and then he heard a faint cough and the muffled plash of an oar. He went to Sir Isaac with the news. He found him still with the captain.

"Excuse me, Sir Isaac, Captain, I think there is a small boat following us. I was watching the glow from the stern and in the middle of the glow there was a blackness covering the light. Then I heard a cough and oars."

"They have come sooner than I expected, my friends. Perhaps the moonless night has made them bold. Make yourselves ready. I will rouse the men not on duty, but all must be done in absolute silence. Let us turn the element of surprise on them."

Sir Isaac and Henri made their way to their small cabin. Sir Isaac girded on his great sword and loosened his new Saracen dagger in its sheath. Henri with dry lips and sweaty palms unwrapped his gift from the smith and made sure of his antler handled dagger as well.

The ship was unnaturally quiet. The captain had whispered his orders to rouse his men in their berths. Silently and efficiently lamps were doused below decks and the tallow candles put out.

There was no moon. The stars were the only light in the night sky. Henri made his way to the stern again and stood by Sir Isaac and the captain who was peering intently into the glowing wash behind the ship. There it was; the blackness that could only be a cutter following the wake of the cog.

"I feel the loom of another ship there in the darkness off the port side. I can smell the unwashed bodies eddying across the waves carried by the wind. Soon they will attack and we must be ready," the captain whispered. "I have had the lanterns filled with oil put into the rigging. Torches are set in the railings. When the attack comes they will be lit. I want to see who I'm fighting."

In the stygian darkness the cutter came ever closer to the stern of the cog. The smell from the other ship grew stronger as she eased closer to her prey. Henri thought he caught a glimpse of the white foam created by the passage of a ship through the water off to their left. Suddenly a grappling hook sailed over the railing and pulled taught right by Henri's hand. He almost cried out, but Sir Isaac had clamped his strong hand over Henri's mouth stopping his shout. The three of them stepped silently back and waited to see who would come over the stern. It was not long before a young boy almost Henri's age eased over the railing like a cat. The captain seized him in an iron grip and silenced him with a blow. The lad fell in a clump on the deck.

Next came an older sailor, eyes and teeth gleaming in the darkness. He too was seized as was each of the men who followed him. By now the upper deck was littered with the bodies of unconscious corsairs, knocked out and bound by the crew in some bizarre assembly line. The count rose to seven before the captain pulled on the rope and felt the cutter lightly follow in the wake of the cog.

"The ship shadowing us must be waiting for a signal. Keep silent and perhaps we can foil their attack."

At that moment a gust of wind brought the corsair ship crashing against the port side of the cog. Hooks and ropes sailed in the air as the attacker tried to bind the high sided cog to the smaller vessel.

"Allons! Allons!" shouted the captain and all over the ship lanterns were lit and torches burst into flame. The ship shone like a beacon on the sea, the glow echoing across the waves making the sea burn as the corsairs swarmed over the side of the cog to the sailors waiting with knives, swords and cudgels. The crew of the cog waded into the screaming cursing corsairs with swords swinging and cudgels gripped tightly in their hands. The battle had begun. The wavering flames of the torches gave a macabre feeling to the deck of the ship. It was as if the world only existed within the glow of the lanterns and torches. All else was black outside the orb of the ship. The sound of steel on steel crashed on the air. Men were grunting with the effort of battle.

Some were growling deep animal sounds as they struggled for their lives. Angry sailors battled with greedy corsairs not only for their livelihood, but their very lives. For Henri it was as if the world of the ship stood still. Time was in abeyance. He drew his own sword and prepared to fight. Near him he could hear the resonant toll of Sir Isaac's great sword as it swung its deadly arc. He glanced toward him and saw a small heap of struggling men on the deck around Sir Isaac. At that moment a wicked face filled his vision. A corsair was on him. All the lessons in swordplay from the past weeks came to Henri's aid. He parried each deadly cut driving the evil leer from the face of his attacker as Henri began to drive him back to the ship's railing.

Henri's young form was taut with anger, strength and fear. As he turned the enemy's sword his attacker went down tripping over one of the fallen. He was down and at Henri's mercy. In his blood rage Henri raised his sword for a killing stroke only to have it suddenly blocked at its zenith. He pivoted, his young face contorted with anger and fear. He brought his blade around again to meet this new challenge. Again and again he brought his blade to bear on his opponent, each cut stopped and turned. Someone was shouting his name.

"Henri! Henri! Arrete! Stop! The fight is over. The ship is safe." Sir Isaac shouted.

Henri came to himself and realized he and Sir Isaac were alone in a ring of sailors. The emotions of the moment and the rage cresting within him brought wracking sobs from his body. Sir Isaac put both hands on Henri's shoulders. "We've won, but I stopped you from killing. That is a burden I do not wish for you to bear right now. This is the rage of fighting. Your tears are the release. You fought bravely and well." At these words the sailors began to cheer Henri. The captain kissed him on both cheeks in an excess of Gaullic emotion. Sir Isaac took the blade from his hand. The corsairs were scattered around the deck wounded or unconscious. Others stood shame faced at their defeat.

The corsair captain was killed in the fighting. The cog's crew began herding the pirates together and tying them up. The captain picked some of his men to sail the corsair's ship into St. Malo where it would be sold and the money divided among the crew and the two passengers.

Sir Isaac and Henri returned to their cabin to rest in what remained of the night. They could feel the motion of the ship as it continued the voyage to St. Malo.

Still trembling, Henri asked, "What am I feeling? I should be happy to be alive, but I am quite moved to sadness."

"That is what I call the 'black dog' of battle. While you are fighting you are consumed with the action. Everything is focused on staying alive, but when that is done, even when you have won, there is a sadness, a blackness that sets in. I cannot tell you why. I only know that it happens. We are happy to be alive, but the energy that went out of us in battle drives us to despair. It will pass. Sleep now if you can. We are coming to a beautiful city tomorrow and you will need your rest to enjoy it. Good night." Henri was wakeful for a time wrestling with his black dog, but eventually fatigue overcame him and he slept. The next morning Sir Isaac shook him gently awake.

Henri rubbed the sleep from his eyes and groaned as he turned over, dragged himself off his pallet and tried to stand. He felt like an old man, or at least how he thought an old man would feel if he had been beaten with rods and dropped off a very high cliff.

"It is the tension left over from the fighting. Move slowly, come on deck and let the sun warm you. Here, have some bread. When we reach shore, a swim will help loosen the muscles. There are too many sharks here in the open ocean for it to be safe."

"Is this what you are feeling, Sir Isaac?"

"It is what I feel most mornings after a lifetime of war. I have learned to deal with it. I hope this will be a rare occurrence for you or at least your aches and pains will come from something less troublesome than battle. Come; look at the island city of St. Malo."

As Henri came to the deck he saw that the sailors moved with the same stiffness as he and began to feel better. The corsairs were huddled in a herd by the starboard railing awaiting their arrest by the soldiers of the city. Henri lifted his eyes to see the walled city with the spire of the cathedral of St. Vincent pointing high above everything else.

The captain had caught the tide and onshore breeze perfectly and they sailed smoothly to the quay where they were met by soldiers sent for by the captain with his new cutter seized from the corsairs. The captain of the cog spoke as the prisoners were ushered from the ship onto the dock, "We shall remain here a few days until the capture is sold and the money divided. We may be needed as witnesses to the crime of piracy as well. I am known here so I do not for see any difficulties. Enjoy the city. As soon as we are ready I will have the cog taken out into the bay. Too many rats, four legged and two legged, here to remain at the quay. My cutter will be at your disposal to return to the ship." The captain smiled as the two travelers disembarked.

Henri's leg shook a little as he stepped on solid land for the first time in several days. He had acquired his sea legs.
Sir Isaac and Henri made their way through the city to the causeway that led to the mainland where Henri pulled off his tunic, waded out into the water and plunged into the waves. Sir Isaac smiled at his youthful exuberance that could fight for life in one instance and splash in the waves the next. Henri came to shore to dry in the sun and began to wonder about eating again.

"Could we find something to eat?"

"Yes, we passed several stalls along the way that sold food and cider. We will retrace our steps. I don't want you to starve. Do you want to sleep aboard ship or find an inn here in St. Malo?"

"Will we have to pack and unpack if we stay in town?
"Yes."
"Then I would like to stay on board."
"As you wish. Now let's find some food."
They spent the day wandering through the walled city. They went to the cathedral where Henri lit candles for his parents. They admired the beauty of the stained glass and like a world-weary traveler Henri pronounced the carvings at Mossaic superior to St. Vincent's. They were given a tour of the fortress by an old acquaintance of Sir Isaac's. They walked the battlements and saw the change in water color where the Rance River flowed into the sea.

There was a large expanse of sand at low tide where oyster fishermen gathered their tasty bounty and others dug for clams in the soft sand. Sir Isaac pointed out their cog floating in the deep water of the channel safely anchored against the tide. At evening they went to the quay and returned to the cog in the captain's cutter shaped like a small Viking longboat. The captain had prepared a feast on board for his crew to celebrate their victory over the corsairs and the sale of the captured vessel. Everyone spread out on the broad deck to enjoy the food and entertainment the captain had arranged. Henri and Sir Isaac sat on the upper deck with the captain. There was a juggler; then a magician.

Finally, a minstrel with his lute told stories and sang songs of love lost, battles won and treasures found. The troubadour sang one story about a baron's wife in love with another baron who lived in the city of St. Malo. They spoke through the upper windows of their houses late into the night and exchanged gifts but were never alone together. When her husband asked why she was away from their bed so late into the night she told him it was to hear the Nightingale sing. Her husband caught the nightingale and killed it flinging its broken body at her staining her clothes with its blood. She secretly sent the nightingale to her love to explain why she could not see him any longer and he embalmed the bird in a golden casket as a memory of their love.

Some of the sailors wept at the song. Some were very quiet. Henri just thought it was a dumb story with a very sad ending. He thought her husband cruel and the other baron dumb for loving someone else's' wife and dumber still for putting a dead bird in a golden casket. Sir Isaac laughed when Henri told him what he thought of it and said perhaps one day he would think differently about Romance.

The next morning the ship set sail for Cherbourg and then on to Ouistreham and Caen where they hoped they could find Henri's Grandpere. The captain gave Chauncey Island a wide berth because of the treacherous shoals surrounding the islands. From a distance it looked like a beautiful place to Henri, but the captain told him it was filled with smugglers because of the many channels where they could hide from pursuit. The cog sailed steadily on though out the day. By nightfall they could see the lights of Saint Hellier Island.

Sir Isaac shared the story of St. Hellier and how he sat in his lonely hermitage and warned the islanders of attack by Vikings so the islanders could hide themselves.

They put in at Cherbourg to trade and pick up more cargo bound for Le Havre. Sir Isaac and Henri went ashore to see the town. "Have you ever been here in Cherbourg?" Asked Henri.

Sir Isaac smiled ruefully before he spoke, "I was here eight years ago."

"Visiting?"

"Fighting, well not exactly fighting because the city was taken without a battle by King Phillipe of France. We were vastly outnumbered and cut off from supplies, so after being presented with an ultimatum the English governor surrendered and we made our way back to England thanking Le Bon Dieu that we were not going to be buried in France for a hopeless gesture. over a city that has been fought over for a hundred years.

And now King Phillip has united nearly all of France driving out the English, the Germans and the Flemish. He seems a good ruler."

They spent the rest of the day in the city with Sir Isaac sharing stories of his time in Cherbourg, but the end of the day found them back on board the cog that felt increasingly like a home of sorts. Certainly, they had spent more time there than any other place during their journey and they had defended it from corsairs.

When they arrived on board the captain told them they would sail with the morning tide and with luck and a good wind they would be in the fishing village of Ouistreham by nightfall, just nine miles from Caen where his Grandpere lived. The news made Henri quiet. Until now it had all be just a journey almost like his travels with Etienne across France to the Mediterranean, but now he realized it was coming to an end. He would meet his Grandpere and stay with him or continue in Sir Isaac's service. He began to wonder and worry about just what the morrow would bring.

The hours passed slowly with the wind sometimes blowing in a steady flow, sometimes veering, causing the captain to wear ship, other times to sail close hauled, occasionally dying all together. With each change of wind there came orders, rushing feet and a creaking of boards as the ship responded to each new set of the sail. There was the constant sound of the waves surrounding them and the cry of the gulls that circled overhead seeking for scraps as they soared with the winds. Henri packed and repacked his belongings that had now grown from a single small bundle to several sizeable rolls. He wondered what Mule would think now that his burdens had become more weighty.

Sir Isaac watched him silently; waiting for the crises he knew must be brewing to come to a head.

"What if mon Grandpere turns me away? What if he wants nothing to do with me?"

"That would certainly be to his detriment, Henri, but it would say more about him than you. You are a fine young man. You are very talented. You are brave. You are smart. You are far more experienced in life than many twice your years. Yes, you are young, but there will always be a place for someone with your gifts, your talent and your spirit. You need not fear about your future. Le Bon Dieu is in control of that. He knows your future."

"I have not told you about my parents. Mon Grandpere did not want ma Mere to marry mon Pere. She ran away and secretly by a priest they were married. Mon Grandpere gave her up. He disowned her. I heard my parents speak of it often when I was younger and in the fever of dying, ma Mere cried out to her father and asked him to forgive her and in her delirium he would not. Then she died. Mon pere became very bitter before his time to go and he died with a curse upon his lips for mon Grandpere."

"But that has nothing to do with you, Henri. You are not guilty of the sins of your father. If your Grandpere cannot forgive the past, that is his difficulty, not yours."

Henri stared out at the open sea as it washed by them. He nodded his head, but still his hands gripped the rail until his knuckles were white with strain and silent tears coursed down his cheeks to be blown away by the wind, the salt of his tears mixing with the salt of the sea and still the ship sailed ever closer to his future.

CHAPTER 8

Finally the small lights of Ouistreham came into view on the edge of the sea. They drew ever closer with each passing mile of water. The wind had shifted once again to the offshore breeze of the evening and the cog sailed as close hauled to the wind as the captain could make her traversing the zigzag course going miles back and forth for each mile gained toward the shore. Henri watched the lights of the fishing village go out one by one until only those for navigation were shining in the darkness of the late summer eve. When the cog was within hailing distance of the shore the captain dropped anchor and furled the sail.

"We will anchor here for the night. The fishing fleet will be off just before dawn, perhaps then you may have some news of your Grandpere, Henri. In a village this small, someone will know of him." Henri spent a restless night on his pallet on deck watching the stars move through the ink of nightfall until the first fingers of dawn began to stretch from the shore out over the sea. He could hear the muted voices of the fishermen carrying across the water as they prepared to go out for the day. He even wondered if his Grandpere was among them. "Was he still fishing? How old was he? Was he so rich that he sat in comfort in Caen while others went out in the fishing fleet he owned?

Finally he heard the captain call to the fishermen who were nearest to the cog.

"Vous connaissez Monsieur Tavel? Do you know Monsieur Tavel?"

"Oui. Yes," came the answer across the water.

"Où il se trouve? Where may he be found?"

"A terre. On shore."

Henri's heart froze when he heard these words, but the captain thanked the fishermen and gave orders for his cutter to be lowered for Henri and Sir Isaac. They quickly got over the side and into the cutter. The animals would be unloaded at the quay.

"When the fishermen are out of the way I shall sail into the harbor and tie up at the quay. You may find me there until the tide turns and we depart for Le Hague. I will watch over your animals."

Sir Isaac nodded his thanks and the cutter began to pull for the shore. As they drew near the small quay they saw a solitary figure wrapped in a flowing cloak staring out to sea with a hand in the air as if in benediction. The sailors came quietly alongside the quay and Sir Isaac and Henri stepped up the sea ladder onto the weathered planks worn smooth by salt and sand. With their landing the silent figure turned at their approach.

The two travelers saw a man a bit older than Sir Isaac, but not by much. In the predawn light the man's face shone brown and weathered by the sun. He stood straight, not bowed. His salt and pepper hair blew this way and that with the capricious breeze. His eyes were the clearest blue and Sir Isaac knew he had seen them before in Henri's countenance.

"Monsieur Tavel?"

"Oui, Monsieur Chevalier."

"Je suis Chevalier Isaac and ce jeune homme est votre petit fils. I am Sir Isaac and this young man is your grandson."

Tears welled up in the eyes of the older man as he sank to his knees and held out his arms. "Oh, Le bon Dieu, vous l'avez amené à me, you have brought him to me. Long have I prayed for this moment and each day as I send my fleet out to sea I pray for their safety and for that which was lost to return to me. Come mon petit fils."

Henri rushed to the open arms of his Grandpere and buried his face into his shoulder as his own tears started from his eyes. Sir Isaac knew their journey was complete. The lost boy was found.

THE END!

Author's Note

There were several crusades labelled "Children's Crusades." The Crusade in this story was let by a young man from Cluny and he believed that when he and his followers reached the Mediterranean Sea it would open up and they would be able to walk across on dry land to the Holy Land. History estimates that there were about 30,000 children, teens and adults that comprised this Crusade. There were no knights, no soldiers, no Church leaders. It was largely peaceful in intent. When they reached the sea and it did not part Etienne of Cluny left his followers, returned to his home and lived the rest of his life seeking to help others and serving God as best he knew how. His followers were desolated and angry. I think Etienne was a sincere young man who truly believed in what he was doing, but he was very young.

The history of this story is accurate. There was a religious war going on in France that devastated the country side. There is a tidal bore on the Garran River.

The cathedral at Mossaic was one of the finest in its day and was a part of the pilgrim path from France into Spain over the Pyrenees Mountains drawing thousands of faithful pilgrims touring on foot, carriage or horseback.

St. Malo was infamous in its day for pirate attacks on shipping.

The Hospital of St. John at Marseilles was destroyed by time and tide. It is described in a number of very old histories as a place of help and comfort to the sick.

While this is a work of fiction, I have tried to paint as accurate portrayal of the times, the weapons, the places, the clothing the culture, the boats, the architecture and the people as I am able. Life in the Middle Ages was hard.

Grace and peace be with you,
Doug Whitley